Soup Pot

Soup Pot

*Stories for All Seasons
for Children of All Ages*

ETHEL POCHOCKI

Illustrations by
Mary Beth Owens

Resurrection Press
Mineola • New York

First published in 1996 by Resurrection Press, Ltd.
P.O. Box 248
Williston Park, NY 11596

ISBN 1-878718-33-9
Library of Congress Cataloging-in-Publication No. 96-68371

Cover design by John Murello
Cover illustration by Mary Beth Owens

Printed in the United States of America.

Contents

Foreword

Nothing touches the heart like a good story, and all good stories come from the heart. Dostoyevsky knew all about it when he gave us a socko story within a story, "The Grand Inquisitor" in the course of *The Brothers Karamazov.* Will Rogers understood this when for many years in his syndicated newspaper column he told a nation the story he heard the nation telling him. So deeply did Will Rogers touch this nation's heart that when he died in a tragic airplane accident in 1935 the news struck the people, coast to coast, almost literally dumb; it can only be compared for a later generation to the impact of John F. Kennedy's assassination in 1963. Thus do we love our greatest storytellers, and thus do we mourn their passing.

Garrison Keillor — not only a terrific storyteller but a superb folk theologian — knows the power of stories to touch and shape the heart as he narrates his accounts on public radio of events in his mythical Minnesota home town of Lake Wobegon. The ordinary events in the lives of the citizens of that imaginary burg constitute the stories of our lives, too — lives both ordinary and sacred. When we hear their stories we hear our own stories, and we laugh, and we cry, and we want more than ever to go on living.

Where would we be without our storytellers and their stories? A culture intellectually, morally, and spiritually enslaved by the video media craves a good story. Stories told are one thing, of course, and stories written are another. The oral tradition grows, changes, is dynamic, taking on new directions, different shadings as the storyteller is moved and the listening community requires. To put a story into words on paper is to cast it in a form that allows us to hold the story in our hands, to go back over its words and sentences, to read them at our own pace and in our own good time. To write a story down for people to read allows us to examine the story and reflect on it as the spoken story cannot do.

Ethel Pochocki of Maine has a special gift for writing stories that are at once simple, sometimes startling, often witty, but always likely to touch you deeply — from her page to your heart. Ethel's stories come from a life lived in trust, in faith, in tune with the holiness of the ordinary and the glow of the everyday. Ethel doesn't "make up" her stories, I think. I imagine she allows them to tell themselves through her. Yes. Perhaps Ethel Pochocki stories drift about, hither and thither, someplace in the Milky Way, waiting, waiting, until she takes a moment, sits down at her typewriter, and clacketty-clack go the keys. Then whap! another Ethel story goes down on the page. Quietly amazing.

The word becomes inky flesh on the page in Ethel's typewriter. Clacketty-clack, and we are the lucky ones who get to enjoy the results in a book such as this one.

As a writer myself, I know something of the joy when just the right words go down on the page. Sometimes it can be a feeling of sheer delight. This being so, and Ethel Pochocki's stories being what they are, I sometimes think she must spend much of her time at the typewriter in a state of near ecstasy. My realistic side knows, of course, that such stories don't just happen, not most of the time. A good story takes more than a modicum of hard work. That Ethel's stories read so easily is a tribute to the hard work she puts into them. As they say, ten percent inspiration, ninety percent perspiration. As they say. Ah well. Ethel does the work, we get the delight.

Write on, Ethel. Clacketty-clack.

MITCH FINLEY

A Rabbi Once Said

if you would live
eternally,
write a book,
have a child,
plant a tree.

o lucky me
to have done all three!
to have borne fruit
I will not eat
yet will attest
to undreamed of kin
who turn the page,
touch the skin,
pluck the plum,
that I once lived
and left a wake
of truth and beauty.

—Ethel Pochocki

- January -

Soup Pot

Once upon a time there was a great commotion in the kitchen caused by certain vegetables who could not get along with each other. All day long they muttered and grumbled and sputtered and mumbled. Soon the sound of the bickering grew as loud as a swarm of angry hornets preparing for battle.

This upset the old woman who lived there, for she believed that there had to be harmony in the kitchen while she cooked. If food was not prepared with love, she said, it would give you hiccoughs. It would make you sneeze so hard you would see green balloons before your eyes. You would trip on your shoelaces while playing hopscotch, and, worst of all, the last page of the exciting story you are reading would be missing.

So you can understand why she was upset. The old woman knew full well what the trouble was. Each vegetable felt that he was the best possible vegetable in the kitchen — no, the whole *world* — and saw no need to be friendly with any of the others.

The carrots bunched together in their orange plastic bag. The peas shut themselves up in their pods (except for the telephone peas who gossiped up and down the vine when they were growing and couldn't stop the habit now), and the purple and green cabbages put their heads together in the bushel basket.

The onions, who were a weepy sort, braided each other's hair, burrowed into their brown shawls, and hung in a clump over the kitchen stove. They felt awkward and bumbling, country cousins to their fancy relatives, the shallots and scallions and chives, who minced about being elegant.

The potatoes huddled together in grumpy groups, poking each other with their horny eyes and laughing coarsely. They couldn't care less about the scabs of dirt on their skin.

The rutabaga considered himself the king of the kitchen and threw his weight around quite a bit. "Nothing," he boomed, "can beat my strength, my fortitude, my flavor in a boiled dinner!"

There were a few vegetables who tried to be friendly. The younger lima beans did make friends with the young corn kernels and they played a game of Succotash together in the old black pot. The parsley would fight with no one, shrugged her shoulders, and sprigged off into a jig. When she was not dancing, she was curling with her friend, Sweet Savory, using a dried strawflower broom. She was the best-natured of the lot, adding her opinion only when she was asked.

Not so the celery, who thought himself the brain of the kitchen. He stalked about, giving orders here and there in a crisp you'd-better-obey-me voice, the tops of his leaves waving like plumes in a soldier's helmet.

The cauliflower of course knew better. She was not only the smartest but the fairest of them all. What could be more beautiful than her head of snowy white flowers? Nothing!

The only thing the vegetables did have in common was their contempt for Leftovers. Leftovers were poor unfortunates who lived in the shunned community of bowls and jars and plastic bags in the refrigerator. "Foreigners!" the vegetables called them scornfully, "Has-beens!"

"At least *we* are alive and out in the world," sniffed the delicate French bean, "even if we can't *all* be as lovely as *some* of us."

Well, on this particular day, the Leftovers had nothing to do with the commotion. It was all the vegetables' doing, but it was hard to tell just how it began. Perhaps the potato had accidentally bumped into the rutabaga, knocking him topsy turvey. Perhaps the peas had rolled underfoot of Sweet Savory as she was jigging *Speed the Plow*. Perhaps the corn, playing leapfrog with the lima bean, had plopped into the squashy lap of the tomato. Whatever had started it, the old woman decided it was up to her to end it.

She rapped her wooden spoon smartly on the side of the big black pot. "Silence, do you hear. Attention, I want your complete attention, all of you. I will have no more of this behavior. The air is so sour now, it would curdle the sweetest milk. This cannot be. We are all here for the same reason — to create something of beauty."

The vegetables stopped murmuring long enough to look puzzled. "And each of us needs the other," the old woman went on. "We cannot create out of nothing or we would be like the good God who made us. An artist needs his paint. A writer must have his pen. A musician must have his fiddle. A cook needs her soup pot — and you!"

"Are you not ashamed? Why are you so rude to each other? In truth, there is not one of you who is as perfect as he thinks." The old woman, even though she was annoyed, tried to soften her sharp words. "Look at yourselves with clear eyes."

The woman was right. They were far from perfect. The carrots were covered with long stringy hairs and spotted with worm holes. The rutabaga was so rubbery, a child could bounce it as a ball. The cauliflower's white head was splotched with grey and the broccoli flowers were blossoming yellow. The celery was limp and pale from spending time in the back of the refrigerator where he had been shoved with jars of mustard and horseradish.

"Now," the woman said gently, "if you were in someone else's kitchen, you might be called garbage and be thrown out for the pigs. But Leonie will not throw you out. Together we shall work magic and create a soup fit for the saints. But we must work together."

"You there, celery, stop feeling sorry for yourself and don't slouch. Pull yourself together, onions, and peel off those dowdy clothes — let me see your fresh shiny faces. A haircut is in order for you, friend cauliflower, and never mind, carrot, a close shave with the peeler and you'll be as smooth as ever. Careful there, peas, two at a time, watch the edge of the table — and stop that whispering!"

The harsh wind howled and beat at the rain-splattered windows. But all was warm and cheery inside as the old woman filled the pot full of cold water and laid a bone with no meat on it at the bottom of the pot. She dropped in a handful of barley and then one of brown rice and watched them settle around the bone like pebbles which sink to the ocean floor.

Then she chopped and diced and minced and peeled and shredded and slivered until she had shaped a large mound on the table. The heap of vegetables looked as pretty as a pile of confetti and smelled as good as a summer salad.

Gone were the wrinkled, rubbery coarse skins and the bumps and scabs and spots of mold. The old woman dumped the vegetables lovingly into the simmering water and watched it cook down to a golden thickness.

Finally, she went to the refrigerator and brought

out the Leftovers and added them to the soup. A cup-
ful of macaroni and cheese, a small bowl of red chili
beans, 2 and ½ frankfurters, one Swedish meatball, and
4 brown mushrooms, whose eyes were hidden under
their caps — into the pot they went. Then the old woman
ironed pillow cases and hummed to herself until the sun
went down and her husband came home.

She filled two brown bowls with the soup and
tossed a handful of dried crusts of bread on top of them.
Her husband sipped the soup slowly, his eyes closed, and
continued until the bowl was clean. He left not a chili
bean or scrap of celery at the bottom.

"Ah, Leonie," he sighed, "what an artist you are!
You have created a masterpiece. What a lucky man I
am!" He reached for her reddened hand and kissed her
knuckles which smelled of onion and savory.

"True, true," she agreed, as she got up to fill the
bowls again. "But I did have a little help..." and she
smiled at the pot.

And all the vegetables in the pot knew she was
talking about them.

- February -

True Love Never Dies

One bitter cold night, the worst of the winter, Jack Frost or some other itinerant artist who worked in ice, outdid himself on the porch windows of a farmhouse.

While the world slept, he created an exhibit which would have made any city gallery proud. On nine windows were paintings of the commonplace — snowflakes, pine trees, ivy scrolls, lacy ferns — but in each of the three remaining windows, huddled together in a triptych, there was a story.

In the center window, a tall, princely man with a plume in his helmet looked down upon a slender woman, lovely in her billowing gown. He asked her to dance; she agreed. They clung to each other as they danced, he stiff and proper, she leaning back somewhat, savoring the moment. The first streaks of sun turned her gown to crimson and his plume to purple. Far off in a corner of the window, a peacock bloomed royal blue.

In the window on the left, a young woman sat at a

small table by a window, writing on a piece of paper. A white cat sat on the edge of the table, contemplating the lace curtains frozen in motion.

In the window on the right, two angels flew to Heaven arm in arm, leaving a flurry of doves and stars in their wake.

When morning came, the children, their eyes still cob-webbed with sleep, their fingers turning blue with cold, stood in speechless delight at the panorama. They had to be coaxed into the warm kitchen to eat their oatmeal with cream and brown sugar crusting on it. "Don't worry," their mother said, "it's so cold outside, they'll still be there when you're done."

But she had forgotten how strong the sun could be, even in winter, and how snowflakes melt in a flash on the tongue. As the children ate, the handsome young couple whirled together one last time in a blur of brilliant color, until their bodies melted into a trickle which spilled over onto the window sill. "Never fear, my darling," cried the young man while he still had a face, "true love never dies!"

The angels, shining like gold now, knew they would not reach Heaven, but, being angels, they just laughed merrily and waved good-bye to the stars and doves, who were already fading. "Don't worry, my dears, we'll all be back. True love never dies!"

In the picture with the writer, the lace curtains went first, sparkling as if they had been strung with sequins, and then the cat, as if he had just slipped from the table. The young woman barely had time to finish her letter to her beloved — "Dearest, no matter what, true love never dies!" — before everything, desk, paper, inkwell, the young woman, disappeared.

The pictures were soon forgotten by the children, now eager to rush outside and leave their mark on the untouched snow. The daylight world of snowplows and mailboxes and barking dogs shone bright and clear through windows now cleared of all enchantment.

Many months later in the summer, if the children looked closely at a patch of meadow flowers beyond the garden, they might have seen a slender poppy in a scarlet kimono, dancing with a stalwart thistle of such regal bearing, he towered above all other flowers. The dancers regarded each other so tenderly that the butterflies lined up to watch and refused to bother them for nectar.

And below the meadow in the apple orchard, they would have seen two newlywed doves in their nest, singing soft, sad songs to each other and then they would dash off for a carefree soaring, playing hide-and-seek and follow-the-leader. Such activity was unusual for doves, but then, they were newlyweds.

As they swept through blossoming apple trees, they set off a petal fall of fragrant snow, which the wind caught and tossed like stars to the sky. Doused with petals, the doves cooed, "Never have two doves, two *anything*, been so in love!"

And if the children had looked up at the farmhouse, they might have seen their sister, a budding poet, writing at the table by her bedroom window, staring past the curtains, searching for a perfect word. She wrote with a quill pen, the feather tickling her chin, which she dipped into an inkwell, then held the pen poised in air, ready for inspiration, should it come. A black kitten sprawled on the edge of the table, trying to knock over the inkwell.

The sheet of paper before her contained one line: *A thing of beauty is a joy forever.* She thought this an appropriate subject for a summer's day, even though she suspected it wasn't an original thought.

She looked past the lace curtains and the black cat to see the dancing flowers and the flurry of petals stirred up by the giddy doves, and the sweetness of it all poured out through her pen.

Out of nowhere, as if some angel had dropped the words into her mind, the young woman wrote and underlined: *True Love Never Dies,* which, she reasoned, was *almost* the same as *A Thing of Beauty Is a Joy Forever.*

Her pen kept dipping and writing, as if it had a mind of its own, and before she knew it, the sheet of paper was covered with swirls and flourishes and i's dotted with tiny circles. She was quite proud of what she had written and how it looked on the paper and how all the lines rhymed with "dies" — flies, cries, skies, butterflies — so effortlessly. She knew she had been truly inspired.

The young woman blotted the paper, folded it, put it into a pink envelope, sealed it with a red wax heart, and mailed it to her one true love.

- March -

The Wreath of Holy Thorn

There are many legends about Joseph of Arimathea, that other Joseph who watched over Mary and her Son. Few can be proven, but we do know that he was part of Jesus' life both while he lived and after he died. Some say he was Jesus' uncle; others claim that he was a close family friend, an esteemed lawyer and a good and just man.

He was also a wealthy merchant who made his money in the tin trade, sailing a fleet of ships to England to trade Roman products for its tin, lead, copper and other building materials needed by the Romans. It is said that the young Jesus, and sometimes his mother, sailed with Joseph on these trips, and that he played in the fields of Somerset and Cornwall while his uncle was about his business.

When Jesus grew up and began teaching about a loving God, Joseph secretly believed in Him, but he did not have the courage to admit it openly. What would the community think if he professed belief in a King not of this world?!

But when Jesus gave up his life on the cross, something happened to Joseph. His grief gave him the courage to break out of his cowardice. He went to Pilate and asked permission to bury Jesus in his own tomb, which, in the custom of the day, was already prepared in his garden.

Pilate, whose conscience was heavy with guilt, agreed, hoping that once Jesus was out of sight, he would be out of mind. Giving the man a decent burial, Pilate thought, would show him to be a man of compassion as well as justice.

So Joseph and Nicodemus, another follower of Jesus, carried the body to the tomb and wrapped it in herbs and clean linen. When Joseph sealed the tomb with a boulder, he knew that he had also sealed off his old life. Now he was an open, professed believer in the teachings of a man the government had condemned and put to death.

After the miracles of Resurrection and Pentecost, the apostles scattered to the ends of the world as they knew it. Philip and Joseph went to France and preached to all who would listen. Then, when the time was right, Philip sent Joseph and twelve other disciples off to England to spread the good news.

They landed at Cornwall, where Joseph was already known from his trading days, and were made welcome by the King of Britain. Although he was not a Christian, he was friendly to the group and gave them some land where they might live, an island called Glastonbury in the shire of Somerset.

Here, in this place of lush green beauty, they built their first home and a church dedicated to Mary. At the foot of a large-hill called Glastonbury Tor was the Holy Well, which even today is known for its healing power. It is also called the Chalice Well, because, according to legend, it is here that the chalice which Jesus used at the last supper was buried by Joseph.

He had brought it with him and at first kept it on the altar in the church. But so many curious folk kept touching it and shaking it, as if they expected Christ to fall out of it, he felt he must put it away for safe-keeping. Some say it is buried near the well, or that he took it with him when he traveled north, or that it was buried with him under the Glastonbury church ruins. It has never been found. But that, the quest for the Holy Grail, is another story.

This is another. It is about Joseph's staff, which was fashioned from a Hawthorne tree that grew in his garden. He was never without it in his daily walks and climbs and visits with the native people, who were Druids. With his gentle good manners and his gift for telling stories, he was always welcomed and invited to share their meals.

The Druids were a curious, eager people, full of

wonder at all mystery. They asked questions about this Jesus. How could he be God? How could there be only *one* God? *They* had gods for every known animal and tree. Was this Jesus a magician? A wizard? Could he throw fire bolts to the earth? Did he live in an oak tree? How many children did He demand in sacrifice?

Patiently, Joseph explained how one God was enough to take care of everything He had created, that He was a God of love who needed no killing of animals or humans to please or appease him, and that yes, He lived in oak trees and chalk cliffs and slivers of moon and in every human heart that beat.

Once, while trying to show them that nothing God made ever dies, he plunged his staff into the ground with fervor. Immediately, it turned green and began to sprout leaves. Before their eyes, in the biting winter's chill, white flowers bloomed on it as if it were spring!

Gareth, a young Druid, shivered and whispered to his parents, "This Jesus must be a magician — He works without even being here!"

Each day the staff that was now a tree grew fuller and continued to put forth flowers. On the eve of Christmas, the tree sparkled as prettily in the moonlight as any modern Christmas tree with lights. Joseph and the disciples hung circles of evergreen tips on the Holy Thorn, as the Druids called it, to show how our lives were never-ending and forever green with hope. The King and their Druid friends came and hung sprigs of holly and mistletoe on the tree as blessings.

Joseph gave Gareth one of the evergreen wreaths, and the boy wore it on his head as they feasted and sang and danced to celebrate Christ's birth.

Gareth kept the wreath on the straw mat where he slept, breathing in the fragrance which promised sweet dreams. When the needles fell from the prickly skeleton in spring, he left them there, for their sweetness did not fade.

He wished the Christians would have another feast soon. It seemed too long to have to wait through the planting and foraging and harvesting times to get to another evergreen celebration. Gareth had become friends with Joseph, visiting him whenever he finished his chores of herding and milking the cows. The old man and the young boy spent happy afternoons walking the shores where cold waves licked their feet, talking of shells and stars and Christ. Gareth wondered if the young Jesus had walked exactly where he was walking at that very moment.

One day, as they nibbled on the wild leeks they found in the woods, Gareth spoke his wish that the time would fly quickly towards evergreen time so they might celebrate again.

"You won't have to wait that long, my boy," smiled Joseph. "Soon it will be Easter, which gives us even more cause to rejoice." And he told Gareth about Jesus bringing the good news which some people didn't want to hear, and about the Last Supper and the holy chalice and Jesus' death on the cross and what it meant to all of them.

"How can we celebrate something so sad?" asked Gareth. This would not be the joyful party he had in mind.

Joseph continued with the story and told of the burying of Jesus in the tomb. "Everyone was as sad as you, Gareth. No one wants to lose anyone he loves. But on the third day after, on Easter Sunday, what do you think happened?"

Gareth listened intently as Joseph told him what did happen, at first with a bit of disbelief, then with a smile and laughter, as he imagined Jesus all-dazzling, zooming up into the sky and disappearing into his home in Heaven.

Then Joseph said, "So come along, Gareth. We've got to get ready." Each of them carrying a wooden beam, they climbed to the top of Glastonbury Tor and there built a cross. It could be seen for miles around, a starkly barren, seemingly lifeless tree awaiting transformation.

Gareth wanted very much to share in the Christians' feast, as he had at Christmas. He was a Druid, but he could still bring a gift. But what? A pot of curds or a comb of honey? He dared take no more from the larder. Nothing was growing yet other than leeks, for spring in

England could be as dismal as winter, so he could bring no flowers or wild berries.

Then the idea came. He would make a wreath, one like the Christians made for Christmas. But it would not be evergreen, because that was for Christmas. He decided he would make it of the Holy Thorn. He would cut the youngest, most tender branches and weave a wreath covered with the magic white flowers. Surely this would please a King!

That night, when all were asleep, he went to the Holy Thorn tree. His heart sank, for there were no flowers. In their place grew long, spiny thorns. He had never noticed them before, when the profuse blooms hid them. He sat in the moonlight, wondering what to do. This tree, sprung from wood that had been a tree when Christ was alive, would be of great meaning. No, no other would do but a wreath of Holy Thorn. And no one else but he, Gareth, would be clever enough to do it.

With a small sharp knife, he cut the young, supple branches, wincing with pain. He worked slowly, winding the branches around and over and under into a plump bristly circle, a thing of beauty to the eye but not to the touch. Again and again the thorns cut his fingers into raw wounds. The blood ran down his fingers onto the thorns. Still he kept on. When he could bear the throbbing fire in his hands no longer, he plunged them into a stream until they were numbed by the icy water. Then he began again.

By dawn, the wreath was full and fat as his mother's braids. In the rosy light, the wreath looked magnificent to him, even without flowers. He brought it to Joseph, who held it silently in his hands.

"Do you think your Lord will like it?" the boy asked.

"He is *your* Lord too, my boy. Yes, He will like it. He wore a crown like this, you know. Just as beautiful, just as cruel. Let me see your hands."

Gareth obediently opened them up to Joseph. Tears filled the old man's eyes. He bent down and kissed the boy's fingers.

Gareth, embarrassed by Joseph's emotion, kept talking. "It's a wreath for the cross. I thought you might want to decorate it. I'm sorry I had no flowers... everything is dead you know."

"*Seems* dead, Gareth. It will do beautifully, as is."

They climbed the hill and hung the wreath in the center of the cross where the beams met.

On Easter morning, as the disciples hurried to greet the glorious day atop Glastonbury Tor, they gasped at the sight awaiting them. The wreath was ablaze with blooms. The points of bloodied thorn had burst into a riot of scarlet flowers, ignoring and surmounting the now-hidden lancets. The rising sun shone full upon the wreath and cross, bathing both in gold.

Gareth's gift was indeed fit for a King!

Some years later, Gareth joined the Christians

when they set off from Glastonbury for the North. He brought with him the wreath of Holy Thorn, which, it is said, he planted in a grove of ancient oaks in Wales, where, it is said, the tree that grew from it bears scarlet flowers every Easter.

But that is another story.

- April -

Crystal Heart

There once was a crystal heart who shared a windowsill with a starfish, a periwinkle shell, a driftwood loon, and a beggarman carved from wood.

The heart was very small, about the size of a pinkie fingernail, and hugged the window lock so it wouldn't lose its balance. It had already suffered one crash which altered its life. Originally, it had been a suncatcher. Every afternoon at 4 p.m., when the sun came around the house and settled in the den, the heart caught its rays and sent shatters of rainbows onto the ceiling and floor and every nook of the room. You'd never think such a tiny bit of glass could hold so many colors.

But then a bored cat began to bat the heart back and forth on its string, and it fell and was chipped. Its owner placed it in the window with his other treasures, all of whom ignored the newcomer. They resented the heart who, despite its flaw, still worked its magic with the sun in the afternoon.

The beggarman, jealous of losing attention, glowered but said nothing. The periwinkle paid it no heed at all and kept on dreaming of basking in the sun on the sand. The starfish *really* didn't like the heart at all and showed it. The heart, knowing these things, sat quiet and wary, not trusting any of them.

The starfish grew so envious of the crystal's daily magic show, he would have turned green if he could. But he said nothing, just stood against the window with his arms flung out like a frightened gingerbread man with a dunce cap on his head. He knew he was just a curiosity. He had no charm or power to turn the sun into colors. To keep the respect due him, he decided he must do away with the heart, so he plotted and planned and used every chance to move closer to it.

When a sudden windstorm took hold of the window and rattled it, the starfish moved closer to the lock. The heart, sensing his plan, hugged tight to the lock.

Then a huge gust shook the panes so hard, everything fell. The loon and the beggarman went down headfirst together into the wastebasket. The periwinkle, still sleeping, rolled onto the desk, upside down. The starfish fell to the floor and split into seventeen pieces. And the heart also tumbled onto the desk, into a shallow bowl of pebbles and water on which rested six brown-skinned bulbs.

"Oh, what has happened to me?" thought the heart as it sank. "Where am I? What is this dark pit? I am covered with rocks and water and at the mercy of those ugly brown monsters above me. Shall I ever see the sun again?" Then it rallied, looking for hope. "No, the man will find me, I know he will. He will search for his maker of rainbows until he finds me."

But the big brown things were a worry. What *were* they? Why did they just sit there and do nothing? The crystal could not know that they *were* doing something. Whenever the man watered the pebbles, the bulbs set out small, groping white roots deeper and deeper, while the green life within their papery coats grew and churned, eager to be set free. The bulbs did not speak to the heart but sang and murmured among themselves of the time when they would come out into the sun and bloom.

"Why, they're flowers," rejoiced the heart, now woven snug and tight into a pocket of roots. Now that it knew they were not enemies, it began to talk to them and tell them its story. They comforted the heart and said it would have a home with them always, and the crystal was so grateful for their kindness, it wanted to repay them. And it knew exactly how to do it.

All the colors he had stored up from his days in the sun poured out and mixed with the water which the roots fed upon. Then, within moments of each other, the skins of the bulbs burst open, and the green stems slowly pushed their way up, past the pebbles, past the rim of the brown bowl, up to the window and the world beyond. Buds formed on top of the stems, and soon after, they opened and a sweet fragrance filled the room, as if a woman wearing beautiful perfume had just walked in.

And again, there was magic. White blossoms mottled with pink and orange and purple held court on the desk by the window. They bobbed gently like cups stuck on saucers, startling the birds at the feeder, looking in at them. The man too was dazzled when he discovered them. He could not explain it, nor did he want to. Who questions miracles, he said, and who would believe such narcissus?!

Weeks passed, and the indoor flowers died and the outdoor ones began pushing up through the earth. The man cleaned out the bowl of bulbs and pebbles and discovered the crystal heart at the bottom.

"So that's where you are," he smiled, delighted that his lost treasure had been found. He returned the heart to its old spot on the window sill, and there it sits to this day still.

- May -

Magic Journey

There once was a little girl named Rosemary who was very sick. She was so sick she had to go to bed in the middle of the day and she didn't even care. Her head throbbed and pounded right down into her ears. Her eyes hurt and didn't want to open. Her skin burned fiery hot, yet her bones shivered and her teeth chattered with the chills. And the smell of her favorite meat loaf baking in the oven downstairs made her feel even worse.

Her mother called the doctor, and her father went to the drug store for medicine, and her grandmother gave her a very hot bath with Epsom Salts to make her sweat out the fever.

Then her mother rubbed a minty salve on her chest, so strong it made her eyes blink, and then Rosemary, propped up with three pillows, sipped a cup of ginger tea with honey and lemon in it. "There now," said her grandmother, "the hot bath and tea, that'll do it. You'll be good as new in no time."

Her mother put a washcloth that had been dipped in alcohol on Rosemary's head. It felt cool and pleasant. Then she pulled the quilt up to under Rosemary's chin, and this felt hard and crowding in on her. Her worn book of *Greek Myths and Legends* was tucked under her pillows. Rosemary had brought it to bed with her, for it gave her comfort even if she was too sick to read it.

Rosemary's mother kissed her on the nose and brushed back her damp curls. "Now if you want anything, sweetie, just call and I'll come right up. Try to sleep now."

The door closed softly and Rosemary was left alone. She could hear a dog barking far off and children playing ball in the street outside and they too seemed far away. A tear in the shade let in a small shaft of sunlight and she could see the dust dancing in it. Every now and then the room seemed to move, circling slowly. The cabbage roses on the wallpaper changed places, and they too began to circle around the room.

It reminded her of her kaleidoscope, and for a moment, just the thought of it made her feel better. If she could just reach down and get it from under the bed—

Carefully, she inched her way off the edge of the bed, and then knelt down on the floor. The washcloth, dried by the fever, fell off, and the design on the rug began to move. She groped around until she found the box and pulled it out. She crawled back into bed, clasping the dusty shoe box to her, and closed her eyes until everything stopped dancing. Then she untied the faded, frayed lavender ribbon, took out the kaleidoscope and held it lovingly close to her.

Rosemary had found it when they moved to this

house, among the clutter of boxes left in the attic by the old woman who had owned it. When she opened the box, she knew she had found a treasure. She believed it had been left there just for her. The long triangular shaft of the kaleidoscope was covered with brown velvet and mirrored on the inside. At one end were two large glass wheels, each wheel divided by copper into three sections.

Each section held bits of colored glass, petals of rose and pansy and poppy, sprigs of fern, thistledown, and the tiniest of gold feathers. When Rosemary looked through one end and twirled first one wheel, then the other, marvelous designs flashed by, one opening into the other, never the same, never-ending. She could see swans and peacocks, flying Oriental rugs, jesters and temple bells and teapots exploding into the sky. She saw people, sometimes whispering, sometimes waving gently, but they never stayed longer than a glimpse.

Today the kaleidoscope was so heavy, Rosemary could barely lift it to her eyes and keep it there. Finally she drew her knees to her chest and propped it up. Then she pointed it into the shaft of sunlight, put her eyes as close as she could get to it, and began to twirl. First one wheel, then the other, and then both together. The scene began to grow larger until it filled the room, and although the scene kept changing as usual, Rosemary saw a round gold door in the center of it.

The door grew larger as she spun the wheels faster. The mirrored walls of the corridor took the place of her bedroom walls, and Rosemary felt she was no longer looking into the kaleidoscope but was there inside it. She was running lightly along the glass floor towards the golden door which was beginning to open, very slowly. Finally she reached the door, and as it opened just a bit wider this time, Rosemary quickly slipped through and heard it shut and click behind her.

Beyond the door, all was darkness. Because she was curious but didn't know what to expect, Rosemary walked, cautiously. Surely she had nothing to fear from a place entered by way of a golden door, she thought.

But the mirrored floor she had skimmed over had given way to a sticky muckmire that tried to suck her up when she walked. It took all her strength to pull herself out, and her legs began to ache from the effort.

She inched along carefully, stepping on what appeared to be firmer ground held down by stumps and tree roots. This must be a swamp, she thought. Rosemary had never seen a swamp, but she had read about them and seen pictures of the crocodiles that lived in them. Now she could barely see ahead or around her, for was enveloped in a thick green fog. Was this the pea soup fog her grandmother talked about, she wondered?

Rosemary could feel sweat rolling down her cheeks like tears. She wanted to cry *real* tears, but she was too weak to cry and breathe at the same time. Strands of broken spider web silk clung to her face and hair. A group of sullen, bad-smelling mushrooms seemed to be following her. Everywhere she looked, when the fog thinned, there they were.

"Is anyone here?" she cried. "Please help me, some-one. I don't know where I am!" She wished she had never turned the kaleidoscope wheels.

"Hello!" A small light blinked in front of her nose. "Did you call?"

It was a firefly.

"Oh, am I glad to see you," Rosemary sniffled. "Can you get me out of here?"

"Oh yes, we'll help. Don't worry about it. The Dismal Swamp isn't the nicest place to be, I know, but just be still a moment and we'll see what we can do."

A conflagration of fireflies came out of the fog and settled on her bare feet, blinking on and off, like tiny red and green Christmas tree lights. They tickled, pleasantly.

"Now," said the firefly, "you will walk very carefully, and we will light your way so you can see where you're going. We're going over a bridge now. . . ."

Rosemary, who did not like high places, tried not to look down into the brown water where something was making gurgling noises. She kept her eyes on the rickety planks lit by the fireflies until she finally reached the other side. She stepped onto firm, grassy ground and into a land of incredible beauty.

Everything was brimming with the brightest and

softest colors Rosemary had ever seen. The sky and hills, just high enough to climb easily, apricot orchards, gardens tucked behind stone walls, willow-banked streams — everywhere she looked, she felt welcome to come and touch and enjoy.

The air smelled of sweet fern and red cedar and freshly baked lemon cakes. Rosemary heard the voices of children playing and grown-ups laughing in the distance. She did not know how far or near they were because she had no idea of where this land began or ended.

Then, Rosemary saw a woman sitting beneath a Damson plum tree, shelling peas. She wore a lavender gown with a white lace collar, and her hair was pulled back into a bun. Wisps of unruly curls escaped over her ears. She looked up and smiled at Rosemary.

"Hello there, Rosemary," she said, "we've been waiting for you."

"Hello," said Rosemary, timidly. She was embarrassed by her dirt-streaked face and her muddy feet.

"Don't worry how you look," said the woman kindly. "It's quite understandable. No one comes, through the Dismal Swamp without getting messy. You can wash off in one of the lakes — Icy Blue is nice, tastes like peppermint. You'll feel better then."

"I'd rather just stay here with you for now, if you don't mind, said Rosemary.

"All right, then. You're here and that's the important thing. Do you like to shell peas? I think it's such fun to zip them out and then use the pods for boats. Here, sit by me."

After Rosemary and the woman finished off the peas, the woman stood up and stretched, and Rosemary was washed in the smell of lilacs. "How about a walk around. Are you up to it?" asked the woman.

"Oh yes," said Rosemary. Her mind was buzzing with questions. "If you don't mind, could you please tell me where I am? What is this place? And who are you? Are you the queen here?"

The woman laughed. "Last question first. No, I'm not a queen. There are no queens or kings or rulers of any kind here, or fires or frostbite or flies — nothing even slightly disagreeable. The Dismal Swamp doesn't count. That's just the way to get here. We live in the land of pleasantries. We take care of it for you so it will always be ready when you need it. My name is Flora. It is my pleasure to make you comfortable.

"But," said Rosemary, ready with more questions, "how long have you been here? And where exactly is *here*? And where is *here* when I'm not here? And why — "

Flora laughed again. "No more questions, please. Let's take that walk."

And so they rambled, arm in arm, down paths paved with small white stones, around the lakes and up the hills, under bentwood arches quivering with trumpet vines and hummingbirds. Marvels unfolded one after the other. They sailed under striped silk umbrellas in boats woven of reed and pulled by swans. They picked raspberry candies, the hard kind Rosemary got in her Christmas stocking, growing on wild bushes. They followed a band of kilted grasshoppers playing bagpipes. They caught snowflakes on their tongues, during a gentle flurry, and they tasted like vanilla.

When they passed a cottage made out of fig newtons, with a roof of candied fruit slices, Rosemary looked at Flora.

"No witches?" she asked.

"No witches, said Flora.

They came to a plump round tree blooming with hundreds of small rose quartz hearts. Rosemary stopped in wonder. A tree bearing jewels! And yet, amidst all the other delights, it didn't seem out of place.

"Go ahead," smiled Flora, "pick one." Rosemary reached up and picked the nearest one. She held the cool stone to her cheek. Then, because she had no pocket in her nightgown, she tucked it tightly into the palm of her hand.

Eventually they arrived in the center of town, the place to which all the pebbled paths led. At the heart of the center was an ornate gazebo in which many activities were going on.

Ladies in long, soft blowy gowns and large straw hats were playing tiddly-winks and drinking ginger tea with lemon and honey in tiny porcelain cups. Two young foxes were playing checkers. Each time one was kinged, they would jump up, bow to each other, eat a grape, exchange seats, and resume the game. "It's an old tradition," whispered Flora to Rosemary.

In another section, a concert was in progress. Two matronly spiders in black beaded gowns played harps with almost all of their legs. A frog in black evening jacket and white tie, bowed over the cello as he played, his eyes closed in rapture. A snowshoe hare thumped a tambourine with abandon. A quartet of Siamese cats joined in when they felt moved to do so.

Adding to the music, the clock towering above the gazebo chimed different songs on the quarter hour, and Rosemary knew them all. First came *Oranges and lemons/ Sing the bells of St. Clements.* Then *I Had a Silver Nutmeg,* and *Lavender's Blue.* Rosemary sang along, quite proud that she remembered every word.

Then, without warning, one of the ladies jumped up and clapped her hands, calling out, "Look, the horses are coming, the horses are coming!" Suddenly above them came the sound of whooshing and neighing. Rosemary looked up and saw the blue sky filled with soaring white horses, their manes and tails braided with flowers and streaming against the sky.

Rosemary gaped in astonishment. This was even better than the rose quartz heart. She clasped her hands and thought, "Oh if only I could ride on one — "

"Oh, so soon?" asked Flora sadly, for she knew what Rosemary was thinking. "It seems you just got here. But it *is* almost time for you to return, and what better way for you to go than on your own steed!"

Rosemary was torn. She knew she couldn't stay here, but she didn't want to leave either. "Must I go?"

"It's time," said Flora.

"Can I come back tomorrow?"

"No."

"Next week?"

"No."

"When then?"

Flora smiled. "When you need us. You'll know. *Now* — here comes your horse. Isn't it wonderful how there's always one around and you never have to wait? Climb on and hold tight to his mane. He'll get you back to the golden door in a flash."

"I don't have to go through the Dismal Swamp, do I?"

"No, no, once was enough. He'll fly right over it. Now, dear Rosemary, don't forget us. It's been a pleasure...."

Flora's words fell to earth as Rosemary rose into the sky, her face burrowed into the mane of the white horse. She could feel the pumping of the strong wings through the horse's body and the gush of air that filled her ears as they soared.

It seemed a matter of seconds and then they were at the sill of the golden door. The horse bent low so Rosemary could slide off. Before she had time to thank him, the golden door began to open, ever so slowly, and Rosemary, quick as a wink, slipped through.

She rushed through the familiar mirrored tunnel, tumbling and twirling until she felt she was part of the design. Round and round she whirled, with cabbage roses and the brass bed and her book of myths and the faces of her father and mother and grandmother smiling at her.

She reached out her hands to try to stop the dizzy circling and felt the quilt, which no longer seemed hard and strange. Her head did not hurt and her skin was cool. She opened her eyes, and they didn't hurt either.

The room was bright and filled with happy murmurings. "My sweet little girl," said her mother gently, "you look *so* much better," and she hugged Rosemary tightly.

"It was the hot bath and ginger tea," said her grandmother. "It never fails, never fails. Now let's get the child into some clean dry clothes and sheets."

Her father picked up the book of Greek legends which had fallen to the floor, and the kaleidoscope which Rosemary had rolled over on during the night, and put them on her chest of drawers. He pulled up the shades and stood for a moment looking at his daughter.

Rosemary wanted to tell him where she had been but decided to save it for another time. Then she changed her mind and asked, "Daddy did you ever hear of a country called Pleasant Trees?"

He frowned and thought. "No, can't say that I ever did. Whereabouts is it?"

"I don't know. Well, never mind, it's not important."

Rosemary's mother had gone to fix her a bath with raspberry bubbles. Her grandmother was in the kitchen making French toast, and her father had gone back to reading the paper. Rosemary, still a bit light-headed and shivery, slid out of bed.

She bent down and pulled the old shoe box out from under the bed and took it over to her chest of drawers. She took off the lid, opened the faded tissue paper, and laid the kaleidoscope back into its home. Next to it she put the rose quartz heart, still warm from her hand. She closed the box, tied the lavender ribbon around it, and returned it under the bed.

Now and then, in the years to come, she would bring out the kaleidoscope and try once more to slip past the golden door but it would always close just before she reached it. Yet she keeps trying. After all, if she found the land of Pleasant Trees once, it could happen again.

- June -

The Peony and the Ant

A snobbish young peony who hadn't yet been born felt something nibbling away at her tight green bud.

What is this nibbling? she wondered, annoyed at being disturbed while dreaming of things to come. She was imagining herself already in the world, swishing and swaying in her elegant creamy white ball gown splashed with crimson, with every eye upon her.

Now this nibbling, nibbling, round and round, as if she were a cheese being eaten by a hungry mouse. Fright took over annoyance. Could it *be* a mouse? Some animals did eat flowers before they were born. Even though she was sheltered, she knew these things. Could a mouse gnaw her off her stem and roll her home to cook like a cabbage?

Anger took over fear. She called out sharply, "You out there! Stop that nibbling this instant. You are disturbing my beauty sleep. Whatever you are, go away. I will not be nibbled on."

She heard a tiny burst of laughter, as the wall of her house began to loosen and give way. The folds of her tightly packed gown were stirring, getting ready for her entrance. She was very excited. But what was this thing awaiting her? If it were a mouse, would it hold her captive and make her dance with him?

Perhaps it was a hummingbird, waiting for the first sight of her. She could understand his impatience, but things can't be rushed. He would just have to wait. Now along with the laughter there was a humming and a chuckling.

"Almost done," said a cheery little voice on the outside. "A few more stitches to unravel and then you're free. I can tell you'll be a beauty."

"To whom am I speaking?" asked the peony frostily. It simply would not do to be told when she could emerge. *She* wanted to decide when she would debut.

"An ant, lovely lady. An ordinary, humble, workaday ant. This is part of our summer schedule: Open Peonies, June 4 to 11. When we're done here, we celebrate and follow the humans to a picnic."

An ant! Thank Heavens it was nothing to concern herself about. Part of the green wall had come away and her gown thrust itself into the air, slowly, teasingly, unfolding like a rose, petal by petal. Finally her house disappeared altogether into the underbrush, and there she was — tall, regal, elegant, just as she knew she would be. The first glorious bloom on the bush.

That very day she was cut and placed in a crystal vase with room for only one flower, so she didn't have to share the oohs and aahs of admirers.

The little ant went home that night with the others, tired but content with having done well the work of the day. Releasing beauty to the world was no small thing. Still, it would have been nice if she had thanked him.

But he knew the peony's beauty would soon fade. Her ball gown petals would fall silently, swiftly, during the night, covering the table and leaving her bare. She would be removed and forgotten, like yesterday's dinner, replaced by a bouquet of just-opened yellow roses and baby's breath. And he, the humble ant, would still be here, munching his supper of fig newton after a hard day's work.

- July -

Bonaventure Bee

There was once a bee named Bonaventure who greatly exasperated his mother. It was not because he did not make his bed or eat his cauliflower or run errands when told. It was because he would not go out to play. He was afraid of people.

Bonaventure was a normal, intelligent bee, except for this fear. He was obedient and respectful and was treated kindly at home by his mother. Sometimes, because she worked from sunrise to sunset, she was often short-tempered. She was especially so when Bonaventure got in her way, whining and pestering and popping up suddenly in front of her.

Then she would snap, "For Heaven's sake, Bonaventure, will you please get out from underfoot and go play!"

Or, "Bonaventure, make yourself useful and take the trash out," or "Bonaventure, please go next door and borrow some wax from Barnaby's mother, *now.*"

And Bonaventure would say, "No, I'm afraid. There's people out there. I won't go out until they go away."

61

His mother would answer sharply, "Bonaventure, what on earth are you afraid of? Suppose people *are* bigger than us and ugly and make loud noises. *You* can fly. They can't catch you even if they want to, and I doubt they want to. Don't you know they are afraid of us? That's why they make all those awful noises."

"You simply can't spend your summer moping around the hive. Why, I should be outside right now, testing the gooseberry blossoms, instead of in here scolding you. Honestly, I have a good mind to send you to your cousin Bartholomew's for a few weeks to straighten you out."

Bonaventure had visited his cousin only once and disliked it. Bartholomew's family lived in the woods in a rotten log, on which furry animals would sun themselves. And there were people in the woods, running, yelling, jumping over the log. Their screechy voices gave him a headache.

Bartholomew's family buzzed in a language he did not understand — "it's that Northern dialect," his mother said, and they always seemed to be frowning at him. Bartholomew was not afraid of people. He said he wouldn't give them the time of day. "Just ignore them, cousin," he droned in his strange tongue.

Bonaventure thought he would rather venture outside here than visit Bartholomew again. But then he would remember his friends and start to sniffle.

"Mother, people *are* mean. Remember Beatrice?"

Beatrice had been his dear friend who had been knocked senseless by a person's flyswatter.

"Beatrice is gone because of a people."

"Bonaventure, how many times must I tell you that one people is a person?"

"What does it matter? They're mean anyway. And what about Barney? He died because he lost his stinger in the wing of a people...person."

"They call them arms, Bonaventure, not wings."

"And what about Bertram?" Bertram was a third cousin who had met an unhappy end when he fell into a pot of strawberry jam.

"Bertram should have had enough sense not to go into the house," said his mother, losing patience. "Listen, Bonaventure, these things happen, but it's not always the person's fault. People have been good to us. We have these nice roomy hives and apple and cherry orchards and buckwheat fields, all planted by people."

She smiled, a little wistfully. "I don't know if you're old enough to remember Uncle Benedict. He was my favorite brother. Oh, he had his faults. He was just a little too fond of thistles, for one thing. Crazy about them, couldn't leave them alone, and sometimes, well, he imbibed too much. He could hardly fly straight. He even went home to the wrong hive once, and what a commotion that caused!"

Bonaventure didn't understand where the story was going, but at least his mother had stopped talking about

sending him to Bartholomew's, so he listened with great
interest.

"Well, the people came and cut down every thistle
and plowed the field under and planted oats. Uncle Benedict was crushed, but from then on, he was a changed
bee. He would take the pollen only from thyme. He got
used to it and soon enjoyed it almost as much as thistles. It just shows you, you can do anything you set your
mind to."

"What is thyme?" asked Bonaventure. He wondered
if it was the same time of day Bartholomew wouldn't
give to people.

"Thyme is a little spicy herb. You probably wouldn't
like it. It's an acquired taste." Before Bonaventure could
interrupt, she began another tale of inspiration, "Do you
think Aunt Bernice was ever afraid of people?"

Bonaventure knew that after Uncle Benedict came
Aunt Bernice, and he knew it was best to keep quiet so it
would end quickly. Aunt Bernice was the family heroine.
She was really a Great-Great-*Great* Aunt, but since after
her there had never been another Bernice, it was easier
to call her *Aunt*.

She had lived in Scotland at the time of Robert the
Bruce, and, the story was, she had been flying about the
hut where he lay weary and discouraged after losing an
important battle. He watched a spider finally spin her
web, after failing six times. When the spider succeeded,
Robert took this as an omen that he too must try again.

Bernice so admired his courage, she vowed to stay with him forever. Surely she, a proud bee, could inspire as well as a web-bound spider!

During the Battle of Bannockburn, she clung to the top of his plume and droned *Scotland the Brave* as courageously as the bagpipes on the field. Bonaventure's mother said that Aunt Bernice was the original bee in a bonnet. And if Aunt Bernice could go into battle for the sake of a *person,* surely Bonaventure could change his ways!

"Now," she said brusquely, "I can't dilly-dally any longer. Are you coming with me to the buckwheat field, or do you plan to pack for your trip?"

Bonaventure decided to try the field. At first he flew cautiously close to the ground, so he could hide in the grass if he heard a person. Then, seeing no one, he spread his wings and soared boldly into the sky, circling over his mother but making sure she was still in sight.

Before he knew it, he had left the field and was drawn to the window of a farmhouse, a window from which came a smell so sweet, it made him sigh in midair.

What rare blossom could it be? Could it be thyme? No, this was not bitter. It was the warm pink smell of a raspberry currant pie that sat cooling on the sill. Scarlet juice bubbled under the sugared crust and oozed up in puddles on top of it.

Bonaventure flew through the window and into the

house, where he saw a vase of flowers in the center of the kitchen table. They smelled even better than the pie. He wondered if this was how Uncle Benedict felt about thistles.

He hovered around the clover, foxgloves, lilacs, and settled on a hollyhock. He burrowed into the ruffle, his fear forgotten in the bliss of the moment.

Suddenly he heard a terrible screeching that meant only one thing — *people*. He remembered Beatrice and tried to control his wings lest they tremble and give him away. He held his breath, hoping the hollyhock pollen would not make him sneeze.

"Mommy there's a bee, hurry, *kill it!*" A small person in a red dress was making the horrible noise and hiding behind a taller person in a yellow dress. Bonaventure wanted his mother. Why had he ever flown away from her? He wished he was in the buckwheat field right now, playing tag with his friends.

"Lucy, stop that screaming this minute!" The taller person sounded like his mother. "It's just a poor little bee who flew in the window. See? He's getting a drink from the flowers. He won't hurt you if you leave him alone. Why, you're twice — double twice — the size he is. Aren't you sorry to make such a fuss?"

And Lucy's mother quietly picked up the vase of flowers and carried it out to the back porch. She put it on the step and came back into the kitchen, closing the screen door tight. She and Lucy watched as Bonaventure flashed out of the hollyhock and zoomed into the sky, zigzagging towards the buckwheat field.

"Did you see how little he was?" asked Lucy's mother. "If it weren't for bees, we wouldn't have honey, and you know how much you like honey butter on your toast."

"Yes," whined Lucy, "but I don't like bees. I don't like bees or spiders that crawl on the ceiling when I'm in bed or moths that stick to windows or ants that live under the sink. And I *hate* worms that squish under my feet. I'm never going outside to play again. Never, until you make the bugs go away."

Her mother sighed. She took the pie off the window sill and shut the window. Lucy dipped her finger in the pink juice puddle and licked it. Her mother put her arm around her. "Honey," she said, "you're going to have to learn to live with bees. They have their life and we have ours, so let them go about their business. Will you remember that when you go out?"

"I'm never, ever going out, said Lucy, still licking her fingers, "unless you come with me."

Bonaventure got a good scolding from his mother when he returned. He was so glad to hear her voice again, he didn't mind at all. "Bonaventure," she began, "what am I going to do with you? First, you're afraid to go out. Then, when you do, you're *so* brave, you fly away and leave me to worry about you. Then you come back without even a *twinge* of regret for your behavior.

Tomorrow you leave for Bartholomew's, and that's my final word."

Then Bonaventure told her about his adventures and marvelous escape from the terrible people. He puffed up his bravery a bit and said that Lucy had chased him around the table five times with a fly swatter. His mother said nothing, just gave a few short buzzes to show she was listening.

Bonaventure nudged against her. "But you know, Mother, you were right. They aren't *all* bad. The tall person wasn't even ugly. She reminded me of you. She smelled like daffodils. And she had a kind voice."

"Bonaventure," his mother said tenderly, you are such an adventurer. You remind me of your father in so many ways."

The story of Bonaventure's escape travelled from hive to hive, and he was considered a hero for two weeks. He did not have to visit Bartholomew after all. As a special treat, his mother sent him for a vacation to Aunt Bronwyn, who lived in Bryn Mawr, in a lovely, musty attic.

When he returned, Bonaventure, like Benedict, was a changed bee. With an air of confidence, he emptied the trash, ran errands, took younger bees on camping trips, all without being asked. As for people, Bonaventure decided they did have a place in his world, and he would learn to live with them. As his mother said, he didn't have to like them to be polite.

- August -

Hurricane Flowers

Once upon a time, down in the southern lands where it is always warm, a man named Marcellus lived with his cat, Clara, in a shack near the ocean.

Marcellus was black and Clara was white, and they were both very old. Sometimes they teased and scolded each other, but for the most part, they shared their lives agreeably and took care of each other.

Marcellus was a handyman. He sharpened scissors, fixed lawn mowers, cleaned out cellars, and did any work that needed doing. He was also a beachcomber. Each morning he gathered the tide's bounty — scallop shells, colored bottles, satiny driftwood — and sold it at market.

Everyone in town knew Marcellus and Clara and liked them. He had a gentle, joyful way about him that made everyone feel good. Even if they had no work for him, they sent him home with cornbread or catfish or soft bananas.

Marcellus and Clara had enough to eat, even without these gifts. They went berrying and picked peach drops and caught crabs and cooked them over a fire on the beach at night. Then Marcellus would swim in the warm ocean, which soothed his stiff bones and washed away the day's dust. Clara washed herself in her own bathing ritual, occasionally stopping to watch him sing and splash. She could not imagine doing such a thing, but then, she remembered, he was a human.

And then they went to sleep in a shack which Marcellus had built out of driftwood, lumber scraps, tarpaper and cardboard. The bricks for the chimney he salvaged from the fireplace of an abandoned house. To everyone else, the shack may have seemed an eyesore. To Marcellus and Clara, it was a comfortable, snug home.

It was painted lavender, because the owner of the hardware store had given Marcellus the paint, and its small window was covered with bits of glued-on beach glass. When the sun glinted right on the mixture of scarlet, green and blue glass, the room was awash in rainbows.

Marcellus and Clara were *almost* completely content in their life. Only one thing was needed to make it perfect — a garden. He yearned for flowers, a few greens, mint for tea, and catnip for Clara. He wanted morning glory and honeysuckle to wind their vines around the house, and sunflowers in the corn and poppies in the peas. He could see his garden perfectly in his head!

But it grew *only* in his head. Each spring he bought new seeds and plants. He got fertilizer from the farmers and worked it into the small plot behind his shack until the dirt was smooth as cocoa. Then he planted, certain that *this* year they would grow.

And each year, nothing grew. The few plants brave enough to poke their heads through the earth were sickly and soon died or were eaten by unfussy crows.

This year was no different. "I suppose I should just give up," sighed Marcellus, looking at the sorry sight. The setting sun caught a glint of scarlet in the beach-glass window and sparkled. Perhaps his window was his flower garden, he thought, and that gave him comfort.

The air that night was thick and heavy, the sky star-less. He did not bathe in the ocean, for the water was rough and sullen. Nothing moved, no bird sang, Clara's ears were flattened, pulled back tightly from her face, her eyes wary. There would be a storm, Marcellus knew, but that did not bother him. He closed the door to the shack tightly as he could. He hoped it would not be a bad one.

But it was. The wind howled and tore limbs from trees and roofs from houses and knocked down tele-phone poles. The people would talk for years about this hurricane that came in the night and changed their lives.

Marcellus and Clara barely escaped before the wind lifted the shack and tossed it into the ocean. Marcellus' rocker shot through the air and rode the wind until it was dumped into a backyard several towns away.

They ran as quickly as their old bones would take them to a cave where bats lived. Clara hesitated to follow Marcellus into the cave — she did not like bats — but the crashing of a nearby tree sent her leaping through the entrance and into Marcellus' lap. They huddled together, comforting each other.

By morning the wind had gone. The sun came out cheerily, as if nothing had happened that her smile couldn't fix. Marcellus and Clara went back to where the shack had been. All that was left was a can of kidney beans.

The townspeople were as bad off as Marcellus, so he and Clara set to work helping them rebuild. Now and then Marcellus would find a plank of flooring, an unhinged door, a rug, even a bird bath, which no one claimed. He stacked everything in a pile and each day took home as much as he could carry.

He silently wished for help, for it was a long walk and he tired easily, but he did not ask. He knew the others were busy with their own woes. People didn't think to offer Marcellus help, because he had always been their helper. He never showed his need. So he struggled alone with his load. Slowly, their new home began to take shape.

Marcellus and Clara wrapped themselves in a blanket and slept on the spot where the bedroom would be. One morning Clara woke and stretched and sniffed. Something was different. She sniffed again and followed the scent to the garden, which was now a pale green carpet of tightly furled leaves. Clara ran to wake Marcellus by licking his nose with her sandpaper tongue and led him to the spot to see for himself the multitude of leaves in the garden.

"What is this?" he whispered. "What flowers are these? Who planted them?" Marcellus and Clara looked at each other, dumbfounded.

Each day they checked to see how much the plants had grown. Soon the leaves on the tall, thick stems were long and wavy, like corn. The small pods at their tips grew fat and looked as if they would pop at any moment. One night, they did. When Marcellus and Clara awoke, they found a mass of beautiful, strange flowers.

They looked as if they should be in the hands of angels, velvety crimson and royal purple and ivory spotted with green trumpets. Even the beachglass window had not made such a blaze of colors!

Marcellus rushed to town to tell everyone the miracle. People smiled politely, not wanting to hurt his feelings. "Surely you must have planted them, Marcellus, and forgot about them," they said.

"Oh, no," he cried, "I could never forget that! Besides, nothing has ever grown there. . . . "

Some of the learned elders of the town — botanists, professors, and others who knew everything about everything — returned with him, certain they could identify the mystery flowers.

But they too were dumbfounded. They walked around the patch, stroking their chins, pulling their beards, muttering, "Interesting...," each waiting for the other to make the first guess.

"I believe," harrumphed one, "it is a form of *Lavatera Primavera*, normally found in Iceland" — but the others disagreed.

"Ah, yes," said another "it is definitely a variety of *Cinnamona Salmonella* which grows in the mountains of Tibet," but the others again disagreed.

"But of course! It is the rare and endangered *Accordiana Valeriana!*" exclaimed another.

"No, no, I have found this flower blooming in an olive grove in Greece. I would know the *Erratica Sporadica* anywhere!" argued another.

The clamor grew, each voice ringing with authority.

"It is the *Mentholatum Ageratum!*"

"The *Primulata Pizzicata!*"

"The *Diddidactyl Dillywort!*"

On and on they went, until finally the town librarian, a small bald man with glasses and a red bowtie, called a halt to the ruckus. Although his eyes were full of good humor, his voice had the authority of one who would have no nonsense with overdue books.

"Gentlemen!" he held up his arms. "All of you are scholars of impeccable repute, but since each of you is certain he is right, surely we cannot accept one and not the other, can we?"

"I suggest we may never know the true name of this flower. We can only thank the hurricane for bringing it to Marcellus and us. Thus, I suggest that we call it the *Pulchra Flora Hurricanus Marcellanus* — Marcellus' Pretty Hurricane Flowers! What do you say?"

The men looked at each other. Then one nodded, and another, until finally all agreed, relieved to have come to such a happy solution.

The next day there was a ceremony at the garden to make the name official, and everyone came. When the townspeople saw the jumble of discards Marcellus was putting together for a home, they were shocked and their hearts felt ashamed. How could they have let their old friend live in such a condition? Why didn't they know?

They went back to town and returned with new pine planks and tin for a roof and dishes that matched and little windows with crisscross panes and the bird bath, which they set in the garden as sentinel. And they brought pots of shrimp chowder and yam biscuits and gingersnaps and root beer to share with each other.

Finally, the house was finished. It was painted a soft green, and it had a porch with two rockers which faced the ocean. And there was a real bed, with two goose-down pillows for each of them. Clara was so exhausted from eating, supervising, and directing traffic, she tried out her pillow immediately.

The flowers in the garden thrived and reseeded themselves every year. Marcellus once believed no flowers could be as lovely as his beachglass window, but now he knew better.

- September -

Poppy's Crown

Once upon a September's day, the wind from the south grew tired of murmuring through the trees and decided to kick up her heels. Her brother from the north joined her and together they romped through the brilliant sky and jumped through hoops of clouds and ruffled the feathers of geese in flight.

They vied with each other, like children puffing at white-haired dandelions, to see who could blow the fiercest and farthest. They tore the scarlet leaves of woodbine from their vines and popped open milkweed pods, scattering their down into the air.

Then they dropped close to earth and whisked away the hay covering strawberry plants and gleefully stirred up the dirt in a garden where poppies and hollyhocks had just been planted. For good measure, they whipped off the hat of the gardener, who was already muttering at the mess they had made.

The winds shrieked in laughter. They tossed seeds in all directions. What did it matter to them that next spring the pansies would lodge with the carrots and columbines would dwell in the shade of the broccoli? What did they care that because of them, one tiny poppy seed, the size of a cinder in the eye of a mouse, would fall into the garden of an abandoned house?

To be truthful, the house was not abandoned, it was *gone*. Except for several boards of splintered wood, standing guard like sentinels left behind, there was no house. Lilac and honeysuckle bushes framed the crumbling foundation, blooming loyally each spring, as if there was still a family to admire them.

It must have been the mother of the home who had created the flower garden now taken over by wild grasses and Michaelmas daisies. She must have planned it and formed its circle with the white rocks from the ocean, placing it where she could see it from the kitchen window. Often she must have held her breath at the glorious sight of crimson snapdragons and blue delphinium, pink sweet william and purple canterbury bells and mottled pansies with their faces turned up to catch the sun!

In the center of the garden, she had placed a stone Madonna, who watched over her subjects and protected them from blight and worms and children who might pull them up. One of the statue's hands was outstretched and upon it, quite poised and content, sat a small stone bird. Through the years, the Madonna's smile remained unchanged, even though her subjects were now strangers who had come in from the wild. It was a smile of surprised delight, one that said, "Oh, what a lovely bunch you are!"

It was at her feet where the mischievous winds dropped the poppy seed. "Goodbye, little one, here's your new home. Maybe you'll grow and maybe you won't. It's no matter to us!" And they rushed off to the city to pick the hats off ladies and toss them into puddles.

The poppy seed nestled deep down into the earth. The wind couldn't touch her now. Protected by the Madonna, and weary from being thrown around, she fell asleep, and, as the snow piled into a blanket overhead, settled in to her new home.

She did not wake until May, when she felt warmth and worms stirring the soil. Up, up she pushed her way through the ground to greet the sun. Soon she was out into the world, her willowy stem swaying as a snake charmed by a flute, past the dandelions and clover and other hardy regulars who returned each year.

Soon the rosebud tip of the slender stem reached the bird in the Madonna's hand. It began to open, very slowly, and then, there it was! Four blushing pink petals, each marked with a purple blush inside, made a flower the size and shape of a teacup. It dipped in the summer breeze and fluttered its satin gown, like a lady in a Japanese kimono.

For a short while, life for the poppy could not have been happier. She basked in the sun of admiration, for she was a one-of-a-kind beauty. Skunk and deer, pheasant and toad, all stopped to marvel at the unexpected sight of one single, perfect, pink poppy. Even the businesslike fox, who did not linger long, would pause and remark, "An incredible sight. However did she get here?" Then he would trot away on quiet, intent feet.

One day during a summer storm, the wind shook the poppy so hard her petals fell. Some fairy children, out searching for wintergreen berries for tea, spied the petals and carried them off as treasure. They used one as a tablecloth for a picnic, another as a doll's shawl, another as a sail for a dragonfly boat, and the last they stuffed with thistle down as a pillow for an elderly fairy.

But by September, the poppy noticed that the animals no longer stopped to admire her, and the butterflies flew right past her. She felt her body begin to stiffen and her leaves drop off, and she could not bend in the wind as she once did.

"I am old," she sighed, "I am no longer beautiful." Gone were her silken petals, gone the grace with which she danced. Now she was a brown, brittle skeleton. But with age she had gained a crown which the petals had hid and which now sat smartly on her head, turned upward to the sky like a thirteen-pointed star. The poppy knew it was there because she had seen it reflected in a pool of rainwater in the Madonna's hand.

What would become of her, she wondered, when the winds once again turned mean? Would that be the end of her? What good was a crown if she was dead? She had heard, by way of a hummingbird trying to cheer her up, that Garden Club ladies often gathered dried milkweed pods and teasel and poppy stalks to bunch in copper kettles by fireplaces. That would be nice, the poppy thought, to live forever in warmth and the company of friends.

But she knew this was not likely to happen to her. No humans passed by the abandoned garden. "Well," she sighed, "I shouldn't complain. It's been a good life. I could have *not* lived at all. I could have fallen into a horse's ear or a swamp or a vat of sauerkraut." She leaned against the stone bird. "Unlike you, my friend, she smiled sadly, I am not made of stone and cannot live forever."

That night, the night of the Harvest Moon, a hard frost came and blackened everything green and living. The poppy went rigid with the cold and thought she would snap.

Then slowly, faintly, a sweet chattering rose in the cold air and grew louder. Three fairies flew out of the woods towards the poppy. They wore the scarlet maple leaves and golden acorn caps of the Autumn Court, and the frost on their wings shimmered in the moonlight.

They held hands and circled the poppy, singing in tiny, quicksilver voices:

Lovely, lovely
is the wind,

Lovely, lovely
you have been,

Now we beg,
our hearts entreat,

We ask your crown
for Bittersweet!

The poppy, deeply touched by the honor, answered, "Why, of course, take it." The fairies lifted the crown from the poppy's head, and proudly holding it aloft, flew with it back to the kingdom of the Autumn Court.

They dipped it first into a jar of twilight sun, that special gold that seems to capture a moment and hold it there forever, and then in the silver of that night's moon. It shone like a prism, and with it, they crowned Princess Bittersweet, the newest of the royal daughters.

As for the poppy, she did live on forever, even if she was not made of stone. When the fairies lifted her crown, her pod burst and the seeds within fell upon the soil of the forgotten garden. They settled deep down, as their mother had done, and waited for spring.

The next summer, and all the summers forever after, a circle of pink poppies danced and fluttered around the statue. They grew as tall as the Madonna herself, so thick her smiling eyes could barely see through their rosy beauty.

Late Bloomer

There was once a hollyhock who bloomed so late she was the only flower left in the garden. Her mother had already settled into the roots for winter hibernation, which made the hollyhock feel a bit odd and unwanted, growing up without a mother. Her siblings had already flown off with the wind to begin a new existence elsewhere, and she had no friends to share gossip or wind dances or sun baths with. Outside of a few heads of cabbage and a stand of brussel sprouts, the garden was gone by, bereft of past glories.

On the day after a hard frost, a little girl came out of the house looking for anything that might have survived for a bouquet for a statue of Mary and the Child. She picked a few feathery plumes of asparagus fern and a sprig of yellow tansy beads. That was it, she thought, the last flowers for Mary until the first snowdrops of spring.

Then she saw the bright spot of pink hiding under a large hollyhock leaf. It was a perfect, unblemished flower, blooming as if it were the middle of summer. It was, she told her mother, a miracle.

They could find no vase small enough to fit the

tiny stem, so the little girl plopped the hollyhock up-side down onto Mary's head. A special flower deserves a special place, she said. Her mother agreed, admiring the elegance of the wide-brimmed gauzy skimmer with scalloped edges. "Now Mary can go to a tea party whenever she's invited," she laughed.

After a few days, the sunshade brim began to shrink. The hat grew smaller and clung to Mary's head like a pink silk bathing cap. It was so tight it seemed as if it were painted on. Weeks passed, snow covered the garden, and the hollyhock grew even smaller, until it sat shakily like a pink beanie on top of Mary's head. "Very soon," thought the little girl's mother sadly, "Our Lady will outgrow it completely."

That very night, the new kitten was on the prowl exploring and jumped up to investigate the niche in the bookshelf that was the statue's home. He rubbed against Mary and his exuberant tail knocked the hat off and down to the floor.

The hollyhock rolled around like a top and finally stopped under a rocker which fortunately was not in use. This was all very bewildering to the flower, who had gone directly from garden to statue and knew none of the perils of life beyond that.

A mouse mother, out on her nightly rounds of picking up some groceries, had seen the kitten before he saw her and hid behind the couch. She watched the tiny hat fall and roll to its resting place, and as soon as she heard the kitten pad upstairs to the little girl's bed, she came out to survey the situation.

She examined the hollyhock, wondering how she might use it, for she was a practical and creative mother who never let anything go to waste. When she sniffed the summery fragrance lingering on the flower, she knew exactly what she would do with it.

The mouse carried it home, squeezing it and herself carefully down the hole in the floor beneath the kitchen sink and then got out her sewing basket and a scrap of white flannel with red hearts on it. She cut it and sewed it into a large heart (large for a mouse, that is) and stuffed it with sprigs of lavender, hops flowers, and the hollyhock. Then she wrapped it in tissue paper as a Christmas gift for her youngest child, who was nervous and twitchy and needed help getting to sleep.

The hollyhock found her new home comfortable and the lavender and hops flowers very congenial. At last she had found the friendship she had longed for in the garden. Once she had wondered why she had been born to bloom alone and unseen. Now she realized there was privilege in being the last as well as the first of anything.

- November -

The Upstarts

There once were two nuns who lived together in a convent. They wore the same habit, prayed the same prayers, had the same desire to serve the Lord, but they had nothing else in common.

Sister Benedicta, the superior, worked unceasingly at being perfect. She was in all things proper, precise, and punctual. Her habit was never wrinkled, her rosary hung just so from her waist, and she never allowed herself to be sweaty or outwardly disgruntled.

Sister Anna Sophie was another matter. Imperfection oozed from every ample pore. She was forgetful, clumsy, bumbling, and as she worked, she hummed snatches of songs, never finishing them. Sometimes the nuns thought the Lord had given Sister Anna Sophie to them to test their perseverance.

The kitchen nuns begged Sister Benedicta to move Sister Anna Sophie elsewhere. She had broken so many dishes, they needed a new set of china, and, when she washed, she always left bits of spinach at the bottom of the pot. And she left crumbs of cheese and crackers out for the mice at night.

The cleaning nuns beseeched Sister Benedicta not

to let Sister Anna Sophie wax the floors. She waxed with such a lavish hand, the infirmary was filled with her involuntary victims.

The library nuns grumbled that Sister Anna Sophie messed up the stacks by shelving books by titles instead of authors. And when she was porter, she let everyone in, including Jehovah's Witnesses and the Avon Lady.

Sister Benedicta would gently admonish her flock. "Now, Sisters, remember — faith, hope, charity. And which of these is the greatest?"

She admitted to none but the Lord that Sister Anna Sophie was her biggest obstacle in attaining perfection, her dark night and day of the soul. She provoked in Sister Benedicta an unseemly impatience in her indifference to spiritual growth. Worse, she seemed happy just the way she was.

It showed in her appearance — she looked as if she had been blown into her habit by a passing tornado — and in her work. She was careless in her placement of silverware, her bedsheet corners always came loose, and her flower arrangements for the altar looked as if the flowers had been jammed into the vases by a blind person. Sister Benedicta often had to rearrange them so they would be more pleasing to God.

It was in working with flowers, especially planting the Mary Garden, that Sister Benedicta felt most fulfilled. She drew the plans, ordered the seeds and bulbs from England and Holland, and in the fall planted them in a circle with Mary at the center. Ten wedges, marked off by white pebbles, spread out from the statue.

Each would bear its specialty in season: Madonna lilies, hollyhock, foxglove, canterbury bells, primrose, snapdragon, sweet william, larkspur, marigold and poppies. And, around Mary, three red lupines.

Sister Benedicta loved lupines best of all. Their proud spikes, she said, ascended to Heaven like cathedral spires. She and Sister Anna Sophie eagerly awaited the first signs of new green life around the statue and within the entire sacred circle.

But when they came, they were not the expected seedlings but weeds. Sister Benedicta abhorred weeds. Their arrogance now in invading this holy place so angered her, she lost her composure.

"Out, you gypsies! Rowdies! Upstarts!" she cried, uprooting them as mercilessly as she would bad habits. "How dare you dishonor Our Lady? Well, *I* won't allow it!"

Sister Anna Sophie watched silently. She didn't mind weeds. True, they didn't belong here, but what did they know? It wasn't their fault. Why were weeds bad? Didn't God make them too? She apologized to them as she pulled them up, saving the dandelion greens for salad, so they wouldn't feel "good for nothing."

She knew that the real reason for Sister Benedicta's anger was that the lupines had not yet appeared. Each day they continued to look for its distinctive finger leaf.

Finally, one morning they found three seedlings, one on either side of Mary and one behind her.

Sister Benedicta clasped her hands in joy. "Oh, the Lupines! At last — I prayed to Our Lady to make them grow and she did! Now we have the Father and the Son and the Holy Spirit all around Mary. Isn't that marvelous, Sister? I *must* write a poem about it." She hurried back to the convent and did just that.

Sister Anna Sophie watched the plants grow taller and stronger. She thought, "I know I'm not very smart, but those aren't lupines." She remembered them from the meadows of her childhood, when she would gather bunches of them for her mother. She knew that Sister Benedicta would not be happy to learn they were buttercups. Buttercups were weeds.

But her honest heart made her speak. "Sister Benedicta," she said hesitantly, "I'm afraid these are not lupines. They are buttercups."

"Nonsense, Sister," the other nun snapped sharply, "These *are* lupines. I planted them myself. I would *never* plant buttercups."

"You don't have to. They just come. Look over there on the hill, see? Same leaf, and soon, same flower."

"No," repeated Sister Benedicta, "you are wrong. Wait and see, I know I'm right." Humility would not allow her to mention her superior knowledge of most everything. Time would prove her right.

And when in time the plants did bloom, all doubt

was removed. Three shining buttery faces waved in praise around Mary. "Buttercups," said Sister Anna Sophie, pleasantly.

"Those horrid things!" muttered Sister Benedicta, "Thieves bearing false gold, out with them!" She yanked the offending plants, threw them on the compost pile, and stalked off, her face burning with the zeal of a Crusader.

Sister Anna Sophie picked up the buttercups and carried them home in her apron. She placed them carefully between the pages of the library dictionary, under *B*.

After a summer of glorious blooming of all the other flowers, harvest time came and the gardens were gleaned and put to bed. Sister Benedicta planted three red hyacinths around Mary. Hyacinths were dependable. And before they knew it, their annual celebration for the feast of All Saints was upon them.

The nuns drank cider, sang rounds, ate carrot cake and plum tarts, played Anagrams, and exchanged gifts with each other. Sister Benedicta, of course, got a gift from everyone because she was the Superior.

Among the last to offer her gift was Sister Anna Sophie. She gave it to Sister Benedicta with the anticipation of one who knows she has created something beautiful and cannot wait to share it.

It was a bookmark, cut from a box of tea. It smelled of mint and chamomile. A green ribbon hung limply from a hole made at the top. Sister Anna Sophie's hands, unwashed from the day's potato-digging, had left smudges on it. On one side were printed the words CELESTIAL SEASONINGS. On the other, three buttercups, leafy arms linked together like carefree schoolgirls, their petals shiny from an overflow of glue, rose from the words inked beneath them:

> *where two or more*
> *gather in My Name,*
> *I am there*

Sister Benedicta looked at the gift in her hand for a long time without speaking. Then she looked at Sister Anna Sophie waiting for her blessing, daring to hope she had pleased.

Sister Benedicta began to smile. She lowered her head and the nuns heard a small, barely audible chuckle; her cheeks turned pink and her eyes squeezed shut as the chuckling turned to gasps of laughter. The nuns stepped back from their Superior, in the possibility she might be having a fit.

Then, her years of practiced self-control rising to her aid, she wiped her eyes, stood very straight, and took a deep cleansing breath. She must not give scandal to her flock, even if she was only appreciating this Heavenly lesson of irony.

"Thank you, Sister Anna Sophie," she smiled graciously, "this is a gift I shall never forget."

She spoke the truth, for she knew that as long as she would rise and pray each day, which would be as long as she lived on earth, she would be greeted by the cheery faces of the victorious upstarts.

- December -

Dominic and the Christmas Cookie-Cutters

In a dusty back corner of the shelf in a kitchen pantry, an assortment of cookie-cutters lived in a cardboard box tied with twine. Their life was quiet and uneventful. They never went out and had no visitors except for an occasional young spider, who, upon investigating, found them of little interest.

Their neighbors — a rabbit cake mold, an Easter basket with pink grass, a grain grinder, a small blue pot for melting wax, a box of canning jar lids — also kept to themselves. You might say that except for the few times a year when they were needed, they also were of little interest.

But once December arrived, the cookie-cutters were brought out from hibernation. The mother of the house took the box down and brushed away its blanket of cobwebs, and it became of great importance indeed. The box was opened and the children of the family laid out the cutters lovingly on the kitchen table, greeting each one as an old remembered friend from Christmases past.

Then began the weeks of cookie-making, when the kitchen smelled glorious from morn to night of ginger and nutmeg and molasses and vanilla, when flour dusted everything from the children's cheeks to the dog's tail, as the mother and her children made and cut the dough with these special cutters.

They were not all the kind you might expect to use at Christmas. Oh yes, there was the Holy Family and angels and shepherds and stars, and the fat Santa, snowman and leaping reindeer. But there were also some very old cutters with handles to press them down which the mother had found at a rummage sale: a large parrot, a fox with brush as large as his body, a British soldier with a pointy hat, a trumpet, and a bluebird.

The bluebird could have been any bird, but the mother called it the Bluebird of Happiness. It was always frosted with blue icing and hung on the topmost branch of the tree near the angel.

There were also gingerbread men — one with a stocking cap, another with a heart for a mouth — and every animal you could imagine — rabbit, duck, cat, elephant, camel, even a seal. Each Christmas the mother added a new cutter to the group. One year it was a butterfly. The children didn't want the butterfly.

"Who ever heard of a butterfly at Christmas?" asked one.

"It depends on where you live," said the mother, determined to keep the butterfly.

"Butterflies are for Easter," said another.

"A stable's too cold for a butterfly," said yet another.

The mother said nothing and gave the butterfly to the youngest child, who didn't know what a butterfly was and didn't care.

By December 24, the cookies were all baked, and the floury cutters were washed for the last time and packed away in their box to rest for the next eleven months. So it went, for years and years and years, until the children grew up and moved too far away to come home for Christmas. The mother grew old and eventually died. The children came home one more time to take back with them a memory of their childhood: a blue and white sugar bowl, a crystal vase, a quilt, a clock that chimed. But no one took the cookie-cutters. Perhaps they simply overlooked them on the shelf in the pantry.

The house was sold, and the new owners didn't want the cutters either. They were tossed along with the old lace dining room curtains into the trash. Boxes of discards overflowed onto the sidewalks waiting for the garbage truck to carry away the old memories. A light snow began to fall and cover the curtains and the box of cutters.

A man came along, bobbing lightly over the sidewalk and smiling to himself as if enjoying a secret joke. He walked as a puppet moved by invisible strings hung from the sky, at the mercy of any sudden gust of wind. His eyes caught sight of the lace curtains. He picked them up and brushed the snow off gently with his large hands. Then he picked up the box and opened it and stood in silent delight at its contents. He wrapped the box in the curtains and holding his newly found treasure tightly to his chest, he continued on his way.

Soon he came to a small shop in a dingy lane filled with other small shops. Above its front door, a wooden sign in the shape of a shoe swung in the wind. It was painted yellow, and its tongue hung loose, like that of a dog. Along the bottom of the shoe, the words DOMINIC'S SHOE REPAIR were printed in round red letters, DOMINIC'S on one side, SHOE REPAIR on the other. Snow was already beginning to cover the letters.

There was a mountain of shoes in the shop's window, a mingling of all manner of shoes that needed fixing — shoes with worndown heels or no heels, flapping soles, nurses shoes, hiking boots, shiny black dancing shoes with sparkly bows and pink satin wedding shoes. From the top of the window frame hung two spider plants in white plastic baskets. They never seemed to grow and they would not die, but they were green and pleasant and asked little of Dominic, so he gave them a home.

Inside the shop, smells mingled too — leather, shoe polish, oil, apples, glue, smoke from the woodstove. Sometimes the supper smells of garlic and sausage came from the little room behind the shop and mixed, not unpleasantly, with the others.

On a shelf above the cobbler's bench, a radio played music from the time he awoke until he went to bed. He liked all music but he especially loved opera. As he worked, he hummed along with the music through the nails he held in his teeth. Sometimes the beauty of it would make him lay down his hammer and wipe away tears with his apron.

When he was alone, he would try to sing along with it. He was careful not to sing when people were in the shop, for the strange garbled sounds which came from his throat frightened them. It saddened him that all the words and joy and beauty inside of him would always be trapped there. Only God would know how beautiful they were.

Dominic had never been able to speak. He had been born mute. His parents loved him dearly, for they had longed for a child for many years and he had finally been given to them. They counted his coming a miracle. If he could not speak, it was a small thing.

Dominic grew old enough to help them and he enjoyed doing so. He moved awkwardly, and he could not write or read, but this did not seem to bother him. His gift was in his hands, a gift of making and fixing things, and in his sunny certainty that the world was good and life a joy.

Soon Dominic could repair shoes as skillfully as his father. The two of them would hammer away, while his father explained to him the stories of the operas on the radio and sing the parts in his clear tenor. And so the years passed, and, as with the young mother, the parents grew old and died. They left Dominic the shoe shop and here he made his world. It was a small, safe one, with its walls the border of his country, and here Dominic was lord and master and content.

As he worked with the shoes, he imagined each one's story. The hiking boots told him of the young man who had climbed mountains in a faraway country. He saw the young girl who wore the pink satin shoes to a wedding and danced too much and lost her heart as well as her heel, and the old woman with stiff bones whose bunions reshaped her worn black shoes.

He liked his customers, who were always polite and smiled at him and tried not to ask questions he could not answer and who even sometimes touched his hand when they paid him. When his back and arms tired of work, he would take a walk. The sight of clouds and geese and playing children, a flower growing in a sidewalk crack, the smell of a vendor's roasting chestnuts or frankfurters — everything refreshed him. And sometimes, like today, he would find something of delight in the trash.

He had no idea what he would do with the cookie cutters. He cooked very little and baked not at all. Yet they were too precious not to be used. As he lay in bed that night, the box next to him on the pillow, a small germ of an idea came into his mind. All night long it grew as he slept, until it was strong enough to wake him at daylight. He jumped from his bed and started to sing, not caring how it sounded.

Today, when work was done, he would walk to the lumber yard and sort through the discards of wood. He knew what he wanted and he found it. He came home with a sackful of odd-shaped bits and pieces of pine, wood that was of use to none but one in need of kindling or an artist.

He dumped the contents of the sack onto the table and lovingly fondled each piece of wood, breathing in the sharp, sweet fragrance of the pine. It made him think of the forests of Umbria his parents talked about. He hoped there were pine forests in Heaven and that his parents were sitting in one now.

He brought out the cookie-cutters and with a pencil traced each one on a piece of wood. Then, as evening drew on, he pulled his mother's rocker near to the fire and began to whittle.

Each day Dominic went to the lumber yard and brought back more wood. Each night he traced and carved and rocked and sang. When every cutter had had its chance, he brought out his store of little cans of paint he had picked up through the years, and he painted. How he painted! No cookies had ever been frosted so gloriously!

To a red pony he gave blue eyes and a peppermint-striped tail; to the gingerbread lady, black hair, rosy cheeks and a purple-flowered apron. A green-eyed fox wore white boots, and a golden elephant sported orange polka-dots. The Bluebird of Happiness he painted blue all over and left it at that — why, he did not know. It seemed right that way. By Christmas Eve, he had finished. Most of his handiwork he gave to the children who came with their parents into the store. His heart did a little dance to see their eyes widen with delight when they chose the one waiting for them. They did not seem to fear him anymore, as they murmured their *thank yous* and ran off.

By evening, the mound of shoes had disappeared and been returned to their owners. Dominic blew away bits of dust and dirt on the wooden platform by the window, lay down clean newspapers, and over them, one white lace curtain. Then he carefully arranged the wooden cut-outs he had saved and which he had made thick enough to stand on their own.

In the center, Baby Jesus in a green swaddling blanket lay in a red manger Dominic had made from the pine scraps. The head and footboards of the manger were formed by butterflies of a species found only in Dominic's mind. Mary, in blue mantle over her white dress with tiny roses, knelt on one side, and Joseph, in a rich brown cloak, on the other.

A shepherd in violet, herding several pink sheep, gazed off towards the star shedding golden rays. Two Christmas trees, dabbed in snow and many-colored balls, stood as sentinels to the scene. From one spider plant, an angel with auburn hair watched over the Holy Family. From the other spider plant hung the Bluebird of Happiness.

A cold, brittily brilliant moon shone upon the scene, and in the darkened street of darkened shops, Dominic's window stood out like an irrepressible jewel. For whom, you might wonder, was this magic made this night, for who travelled here but lonely hearts and alley cats and homeless ones who only wanted warmth?

Dominic did not wonder about such practical things. At midnight, when the church bells rang, he sat down to eat the Christmas bun with icing the woman in the bakery had given him.

First he bowed his head and told his parents how much he loved and missed them. He did not pray his usual Christmas Eve prayer, which was that for a few moments, he might have the gift of speech as the animals did this night. Tonight he did not feel the old yearning, for a part of his gift had been allowed to escape and speak in another way. If his song was in wood, was that not enough?

Then he blessed the good God for the bun with the icing, the pine trees, and bright, laughing color, and, most of all, the cookie-cutters.

And then he went to sleep.